PAIN THAT HEALS

How to Be Delivered From the Stronghold Pain Can Bring

by

Carliss Cole

ISBN: 978-1-4276-1901-3

Printed in the United States of America

Dedication

I want to dedicate this book to my loving and
supportive husband, Elisha Cole
who has consistently fought for our marriage,
and consistently continues to do so, in spite
of all the pain and opposition we endure.

My loving children,
Angel Bethany Cole, and Andrew James Cole,
whom I hope will read this book someday, and
take these loving and encouraging words
to heart.

And
In loving memory of my dear mother,
Gwendolyn Delores Lee, who was my
inspiration and my cheerleader here
on earth, and who is yet cheering
for me in heaven.

Special Thanks

First of all I would like to give special thanks to my Lord and Savior Jesus Christ. You are such a great friend, and a great listener too. You treat me like an individual, without comparison or criticism. Thank you Jesus. Help me in my goal to treat others the way you treat me.

To the precious gift of the Holy Spirit, who is the third person of the Trinity; although last, He is certainly not least! I don't know where I'd be without your help, comfort, and guidance, thank you Holy Spirit, you are important to me.

To the Almighty God Himself: I am overwhelmed by your love for me and mankind. I long to please you and see a smile on your face one day.

To my husband Elisha Cole, who has been very supportive concerning the gifts and callings that God has placed in and on my life. Thank you for teaching me so much, especially how to have fun while under pressure. I look forward to spending many, many more years with you, and enjoying every minute of it.

To my children Angel and Andrew, who create a world within a world for me. When I'm having fun with you two, it seems as though there are no worries or problems that need to be solved. Thank you!

To all the wonderful pastors and bishops who have allowed themselves to be used by God to deliver me in many areas of my life.

Thank you to Clarence and Dorothy Bradford, who are not only my brother and sister-in-law, but also are my friends and counselors, who have been there for me in every situation, in the midst of all my pain, and have also been my on-call babysitter. Thank You so much!!

Thank you to my sister Claronda Odom, who gives me a word from the Lord without even knowing it. You are the one person I know that's not trying so hard to be used by God, yet He is using you. Smile, I love you, and thank you.

And last, but certainly not least, my family as a whole: to the Bradford, Grant, Lee, Cole, Holloway, Troupe, and Whitmore-Loyd families, you all are awesome!!

Table of Contents

Introduction

At first, I didn't know what to say for the introduction. Writing this book in and of itself was a very difficult task; I would start, then stop and cry. I went through a cleansing process of my own while working on this. I had to confront many issues from my own life; some of which, I just didn't want to face.

It amazes me still how God continues to use us, even in the midst of our mistakes. None of us is perfect; so He has no choice but to use imperfect people who often make mistakes, yet He still persists in using us. Not one moment in our lives exists where sin is not present; it's part of our human nature.

> **"Now then it is no more I that do it, but sin that dwelleth in me."**
>
> **Romans 7:17(KJV)**

Some sins we commit, we are consciously aware of, but there are other sins that are committed unconsciously. Those sins must be revealed to us through the written, spoken, and rhema [literally an utterance or spoken word, i.e. *"a word from THE Word (Lord)"*] word of God. Yet He still uses us to preach and teach His gospel, and be a blessing to others in whatever way He chooses.

> **"For no person will be justified (made righteous, acquitted, and judged acceptable) in His sight by observing the works prescribed by the Law. For [the real function of] the Law is to make men recognize and be conscious of sin [not mere**

perception, but an acquaintance with sin which works toward repentance, faith, and holy character]. But now the righteousness of God has been revealed independently and altogether apart from the Law, although actually it is attested by the Law and the Prophets, Namely, the righteousness of God which comes by believing with personal trust and confident reliance on Jesus Christ (the Messiah). [And it is meant] for all who believe. For there is no distinction, Since all have sinned and are falling short of the honor and glory which God bestows and receives."

Romans 3:20-23 (AMP)

I believe we tend to forget this, making it is easy for us to point the finger at someone else and walk with unforgiveness in our own hearts. When we do this, we fail to realize it shows others there is still pain within our own hearts because of unresolved issues in our lives.

Not only do these issues cause us to act out, but they can also leave unanswered questions. Sometimes we do things that are not right or befitting to our true self, or who God created us to be in the first place. Some of us keep on doing the same thing over and over again, even when we know it's not good for our mental, spiritual, social and physical health, or for our well-being. Many times, we don't even know why we do the things we do, yet we continue on anyway.

Well, that's what this book is all about; finding answers to questions regarding pain that causes certain actions and reactions in our lives.

For your enjoyment in reading, the Lord has impressed upon my heart to use a few scenarios as examples concerning different issues and actions that occur in everyday life and relationships. All the scenarios and names used are imaginary. Hopefully they will help you get a better understanding of what's going on in your own personal life and how you can handle those issues with the appropriate response, which is according to the word of God.

My goal in writing this book is that my Lord and Savior Jesus Christ may be glorified—exalted, magnified and lifted up—in the midst of your present and past pain. Once this takes place in your life, that's when you will know that you are experiencing the *Pain That Heals.*

Read and be blessed!

Chapter One

Pain That Affects Your Life

People's actions and responses to certain situations in their lives occur for many different reasons. If we are truly honest with ourselves, all of us at some point have been wounded in our lives in some sort of way. That pain can fester in our hearts and if it's not dealt with properly, it will become sin in our lives. This pain has a tendency to connect with our inner most fears, and as mentioned earlier, how we respond to different circumstances.

This festering, sinful pain affects the way we act and react, what we say and how we say it, and even what we think on a day to day basis. Let me tell you that pain in and of itself is not a sin. As a matter of fact, it's normal because it's something we all have to face throughout our lives. However, pain that's not dealt with—to the point where it lies dormant in our minds and hearts and affects our decisions in a negative way—is sin.

This pain has a tendency to lead and guide us in our everyday lives, without us consciously knowing it. It affects who we choose as friends and with whom we form close relationships. In other words, this pain, without even realizing it, effectively "directs our paths," instead of the Lord directing our paths.

"Lean on, trust in, and be confident in the Lord with all your heart and mind and do not rely on your own insight or understanding. In all your

ways, know, recognize, and acknowledge Him, and He will direct and make straight and plain your paths."

Proverbs 3:5-6 (AMP)

We tend to put all of our trust in this pain rather than in the Lord of hosts, who is the healer of all pain. Even though it doesn't feel good, by ignoring it, it has become familiar; almost like nursing an old wound. When we grow accustomed to the pain, we take it into our hearts and become intimate with it. We may not like it, but it's always there; since it's been with us so long, it seems almost comfortable. We let it in every time it comes knocking on the door of our hearts. Yet, even though we know it will cause more damage, we are not willing to let go of the intimacy with the pain in our lives.

We have built a relationship with this pain. We have meditated on it, fed it, watered it, and taken care of it, like a mother cares for her child. At times, we may push it to the side, only to return to it again at the first sign of a difficult situation. This causes us to create, recreate, or even extend the cycle of pain—in this case, sin—over and over again. As a matter of fact, it constantly reminds us that it's around, leading and directing our paths, making us we believe it's not going anywhere and that we cannot live without it.

This pain calls our name out in the middle of the night, only to bring restless nights with no sleep. It stresses us, giving irritable and weary days. It can take away hunger and cause us to become anorexic, to the point where we don't even recognize ourselves. Or it can increase hunger and cause us to overeat and gain weight, ultimately causing us to become even more dissatisfied with ourselves. This pain increases our desire to be loved and accepted—giving in to the late night whisper over the telephone, speaking to our lonely and longing souls—causing us to fall into premarital sex and adultery. We give in to that whisper, not consciously knowing that we are opening ourselves up to even more pain.

This is the pain that tears up homes, divides families, destroys friendships, distorts our self worth, and causes division in the church and ultimately wars in the world.

This is the pain that becomes sin in our lives. It never seems to go away; but instead hides in us, slowly spilling out, letting everyone around us know, which embarrasses us even more. Yet we still try to deny it. Until...until...we have no other choice but to confront it, face to face.

That's what happened to "Wanda." Wanda buried her pain for many years until it began to come out where others could see it. Now when her pain became noticeable to others, and even herself, she denied it over and over again. Unfortunately, the more she denied her pain and covered it up, the worse it became.

Scenario 1
High School Class Reunion

Wanda was all alone, with her eyes shut, just relaxing in a tub filled with bubbles. She enjoyed taking a bubble bath every once in awhile after a full day's work. But suddenly, what happened on that particular day began to race through her mind. The more she thought about it, the angrier she became.

Wanda: *So what he has a wife and five beautiful children? They're still not doing better than my family. I have a well educated husband who makes six figures a year, and he loves me and takes very good care of me and our three children. So as far as I can see, I'm doing a whole lot better than he is anyway.*

You see, Wanda recently went to her tenth year reunion and saw Bill, her former sweetheart. She refuses to admit she still hasn't forgiven him for leaving her.

As Wanda sat in the tub thinking about their break up over ten years ago, she became even more upset and tears began to roll down her face while replaying the whole episode in her mind...

It was a Saturday, close to graduation time. Excitement and great expectation was in the air; not to mention earlier that day Bill said he really needed to talk to her over dinner at their favorite restaurant. Wanda was so excited and wondered what he had planned. Bill was always full of surprises and that's what made their relationship so exciting!

As the evening approached she put on Bill's favorite outfit. Oh how he loved to see her in the sexy red dress and red high heeled shoes. He arrived to pick her up on time, which was another one of Bill's strengths that she loved. The whole four years they dated in high school, he was never late and indeed was the perfect gentleman towards her.

When Bill arrived to pick her up, she hurried to the door with great anticipation as if it was their very first date. As always, Bill opened the car door and signaled her to get in. Wow, he has such a sexy walk, she thought as she watched him stroll smoothly to the driver's side.

Bill had already made reservations, and they ate and laughed the whole night through, until...until...his cell phone rang. He excused himself, and went to the bathroom to answer it. After about fifteen minutes, Bill returned and sat down. Suddenly there was a cold silence; then began the conversation that would change Wanda's life.

Wanda: *"Bill are you okay?"*

Bill: *"Yeah....yeah...why do you ask?"*

Wanda (laughing nervously): *"Bill, you know why I asked, ever since that phone call you've been real quiet."*

Bill: *"Wanda...I have something I need to tell you."*

20

Wanda: *"Bill, I don't like the way you said that."*

Bill: *"Wanda...I...I ...think we need to call it quits."*

Wanda: "WHAT?!"

Bill: *"Wanda...shhh...you don't have to get loud."*

Wanda: *"I CAN'T BELIEVE THIS!!"*

Bill: *"Wanda, if you lower your voice, I can explain."*

Wanda quiets down, while her eyes fill with tears.

Bill: *"Wanda, I love you, but I don't know if you're really the girl for me. You're the only girl I've ever dated, you're the only girl I've ever, ever... did anything with, and my family and friends feel that we have gotten too serious too young, and maybe we need to date around before we get ….we get..."*

Wanda: *"Married?"*

Bill: *"Yeah."*

There is a moment of silence as the tears begin to roll down her face.

Wanda: *"Bill, what about all the plans we've made? What about..."*

Bill: *"It's going to happen, if it's meant to be, no matter who we date. That's what my family and friends said. They said they want us to work, they just believe that..."*

Wanda: *"I know, we haven't been out there enough, and we may regret it later...but Bill, I don't want to date anyone else, I love you."*

Bill gets up out of his seat.

Bill: *"Wanda, we should leave."*

Wanda gets up and goes outside to Bill's car as he pays the cashier and tips the waitress. This is something she wouldn't normally do. They usually leave their favorite

restaurant together, as happy as they had come, but not on that evening. It was the worst night of her life. Inside the car was a long quiet ride home.

Wanda hadn't seen him since graduation, not until the reunion. How dare he look so happy with his wife, and then have the nerve to bring their five kids to the reunion too? That didn't make any sense to her at all. Well, it was a reunion picnic, but still, at least she had a babysitter. What made her even angrier is that he had the nerve to walk past her as if he didn't see her at all.

As Wanda's thoughts proceeded, her husband Michael knocked softly on the bathroom door.

Michael: *"Honey, are you still in there? You haven't drowned have you?"*

Wanda (laughing): *"No Michael and yes you can come in."*

Michael: *"I don't mind rescuing you baby."*

He looks into her eyes, concerned.

Michael: *"Baby, your eyes are red. Have you been crying?"*

Wanda looks away.

Wanda: *"I'm alright Michael, I just got a little soap in my eyes...that's all."*

Unfortunately, Wanda is a lot like all of us. When her husband reached out to help her she didn't tell him the truth, instead, she pretended to be alright, which is lying. She lied again by saying her eyes were red from the soap instead of admitting she'd been crying.

How many times has Jesus reached out to help us or sent someone our way to help in the midst of our pain and we responded by lying, in denial? We told people we were okay, knowing that wasn't the truth. We must realize that when we reject God, and those whom He sends our way to help in time of need, we are basically rejecting his Word.

> **"For we do not have a High Priest Who is unable to understand and sympathize and have a shared feeling with our weaknesses and infirmities and liability to the assaults of temptation, but One Who has been tempted in every respect as we are, yet without sinning."**
> **Hebrews 4:15 (AMP)**

I believe this passage is encouraging us to be like Jesus. Even though we experience a great amount of pain in this life, Jesus was our example to not allow that pain to become sin in our lives. We must be willing to receive the help God sends our way.

23

"God is our Refuge and Strength [mighty and impenetrable to temptation], a very present and well-proved help in trouble."

Psalm 46:1 (AMP)

"My help comes from the Lord, Who made heaven and earth."

Psalm 121:2 (AMP)

"Our help is in the name of the Lord, Who made heaven and earth."

Psalm 124:8 (AMP)

"Let us then fearlessly and confidently and boldly draw near to the throne of grace (the throne of God's unmerited favor to us sinners), that we may receive mercy [for our failures] and find grace to help in good time for every need [appropriate help and well-timed help, coming just when we need it]."

Hebrews 4:16 (AMP)

According to God's Word, it's obvious He's trying to reach out and help us in many different ways. We must be willing to humble ourselves and receive His help, so our needs can be met.

"Therefore humble yourselves [demote, lower yourselves in your own estimation] under the mighty hand of God, that in due time He may exalt you."

I Peter 5:6 (AMP)

This scripture clearly lets us know it takes humility to receive the help God sends our way. When we refuse to receive this help—like Wanda did to her husband—we begin to lie and cover up how we really feel inside. Eventually our sin will spill out even more, into other areas of our lives and also into the lives of other people.

Scenario 2
Family Reunion

Wanda and her family are arriving at the picnic site at the park. The first person she notices is her mother, whom she hasn't seen in over five years. Now, Wanda claims she hasn't seen her mother because of her busy schedule, but could it really be she still hasn't forgiven her for the way she and her little sister were raised?

As they pull into the parking lot, Wanda's mother begins to approach the car, speaking to her as if they have been talking every day. It's obvious she's been drinking.

Wanda's Mom: *"Wanda, get out of the car and give yo mama a big hug and kiss."*

As she reaches over to hug and kiss Wanda, Wanda pushes her away.

Wanda's Mom: *"Now why are you pulling away girl, get out of the car and give yo mama a big hug and kiss!"*

Wanda slowly gets out of the car holding her nose, because again, just like throughout her childhood, she smells alcohol on her breath. Her mother immediately grabs her and gives her a great big hug and kiss. Wanda wipes it off her cheek, looking very disgusted.

Wanda's Mom: *"Look at you, you're getting fat!"*

Wanda: *"How do you know? We haven't seen each other in over five years!"*

Wanda's Mom: *"WHOSE FAULT IS THAT?!"*

Just then, Michael jumps out of the car.

Michael: *"Okay you two, we are here to have a good time."*

Wanda's Mom: *"And look at my grandchildren. Don't tell me that you've had another baby Wanda. Oh, so you don't have time to see me, but you have plenty of time to do o-t-h-e-r things."*

Wanda: *"Now Mama, don't start..."*

Michael: *"Well, I'm really hungry baby. Let's go get something to eat."*

He gently takes her hand, and walks her over to the picnic table, where everyone else is talking, eating and having a nice time. Wanda's mom follows them while their two older children run and play with their cousins.

Wanda's Mom: *"WANDA LET ME HOLD MY GRANDBABY!"*

Wanda tries to ignore her, but she continues to follow, insisting she hold her grandchild.

Wanda's Mom: *"WANDA…WANDA…I SAID LET ME HOLD MY GRANDBABY!"*

Wanda's mother reaches out to touch her grandchild, and that's when Wanda goes off.

Wanda: *"MAMA STOP! I HAVEN'T SEEN OR HEARD FROM YOU IN OVER FIVE YEARS, YOU DON'T CARE FOR ME OR YOUR GRANDCHILDREN, YOU WERE NEVER THERE FOR MACY AND ME!! ALL YOU DID WAS DRINK AND SLEEP AROUND!! WE REALLY DON'T KNOW WHO OUR FATHERS ARE, EVEN NOW!! SO DON'T ACT LIKE YOU MISS ME AND YOUR GRANDCHILDREN SO MUCH BECAUSE YOU DON'T! NOW GET OUT OF MY FACE!"*

There is an uncomfortable silence. Michael whispers softly to Wanda.

Michael: *"Baby, we need to go."*

They gather up their children and leave. The children are very sad that they had to leave early.

Lil' Michael: *"Mom, Dad, why do we have to leave so early? We just got here."*

They all get into the car, silently. Eventually the kids fall asleep in the back seat. Michael begins talking to his wife.

Michael: *"Wanda, baby, I'm sorry for all the things you went through as a child, which obviously started with your relationship with your mother. But now it's time to get some help sweetheart, so that you can move on. We can go to Christian counseling. I'll be right by your side."*

Wanda (calmly): *"Thank you Michael, but I'll be okay. Maybe I reacted because it was so hot outside or something. But I'll be fine. When I get home, I'll just lay down, because I'm tired, that's all."*

Chapter Two

Getting to the Root of Your Pain

The root of your pain is always in connection with certain relationships or circumstances. Getting to the root can be just as hard as the past experience itself because it causes you to think back on the actual incident(s) that took place which caused you pain in the first place.

Some people, like Wanda, try their best not to think back; pretending it never happened until someone pushes the right buttons causing them to snap, *then* the past hurts are revealed. Yet, even then, just like Wanda, they try to brush it off and make it seem as though what was mentioned really did not mean much to them. Unfortunately, they find more comfort in blaming others or making excuses, rather than getting the proper help to be truly healed from that painful situation in their life.

It is important to revisit those incidents and express what you're feeling. Only then can you release the pain inside in a healthy way, so that you can be healed. "What do you mean, a healthy way?" you may ask. Well, I'll tell you.

"Confess to one another therefore your faults (your slips, your false steps, your offenses, your sins) and pray [also] for one another, that you may be healed and restored [to spiritual tone of mind and heart]. The earnest (heartfelt, continued) prayer of a righteous man makes

tremendous power available [dynamic in its working]."

James 5:16 (AMP)

Through confession and prayer, you will eventually be healed. Unfortunately, Wanda was in denial about the way she felt, in spite of the fact she clearly expressed the hurts and pains of her past in front of everyone at the family reunion. This is what many of us do.

When the Lord begins to reveal the root of our pain, and we truly feel the effects, we start drawing back because of shame, embarrassment, anger and the hateful feelings we have concerning that particular situation. Just experiencing these feelings all at once is painful, so then we try our best to magically erase those memories from our minds, which is not what God wants us to do.

He knew your painful experiences would happen before you were even born. That's why He sent His son Jesus Christ to die on the cross for your sins. However, loved one, you must also remember that Jesus Christ died for your shame and your pain as well.

I want to encourage you right now that Jesus Christ died to deliver you from shame. Some of the pain you have felt in the past or are experiencing at this point is because you made wrong choices that you are now ashamed to admit. When you think about those choices you may hate yourself. When you look in the mirror you hate what you see. When you go around others, especially those who know about that shameful, embarrassing wrong choice, you hate yourself even more. Well let me tell you, Jesus sent a broken woman from St. Louis, Missouri with a tarnished past to share with you that He wants you to be healed, delivered and set free from your shameful past. He loves you and no longer wants you to walk around with your head hung down low, living in embarrassment and shame.

> **"For your shame ye shall have double; and for confusion they shall rejoice in their portion: therefore in their land they shall possess the double: everlasting joy shall be unto them."**
>
> **Isaiah 61:7 (KJV)**

Loved one, God wants you to know that He is going to give you a double blessing for your shame. You must know that Jesus came to heal you from all pain. Don't be ashamed to acknowledge your pain or the things you've done or the emotions that cause you to feel ashamed. Ignoring all of that and pretending nothing is wrong will only cause more pain later.

"But the just shall live by faith [My righteous servant shall live by his conviction respecting man's relationship to God and divine things, and holy fervor born of faith and conjoined with it]; and if he draws back and shrinks in fear, My soul has no delight or pleasure in him."

Hebrews 10:38 (AMP)

It's okay to confess. Admit to yourself, "I am so mad at my mother, father, sister, brother, friend, etc... they really hurt me, when they said or did that." It's okay to admit and say, "I'm so mad at my husband/wife. I feel like I married the wrong person." Trust me, nearly every couple has felt the same way during their marriage at some point. These are just momentary feelings that often come during the most trying and vulnerable times in your life. Many different emotions, whether good or bad, have affected all of us, because there is nothing new under the sun.

"The thing that has been—it is what will be again, and that which has been done is that which will be done again; and there is nothing new under the sun."

Ecclesiastes 1:9 (AMP)

Don't be afraid to admit and confess what's going on inside, whether by talking to a godly counselor, friend, neighbor, family member, or even co-worker, as long as they have your best interest at heart.

> **"Where no guidance is, the people fall, but in the multitude of counselors there is safety."**
>
> **Proverbs 11:14 (AMP)**

You must recognize that those who hurt you also need help because they are hurting too. One of my favorite teachers of the gospel put it like this, "hurting people hurt people." Is that an excuse for them to hurt you or for you to turn around and hurt others? NO! But it will act as a reminder and help you to forgive.

God wants you to get to the root of your pain. Talk about it, express how it has affected your life, and then cry, so that pain can be released out of your system. Don't rush the healing process. You may have to cry for days, weeks, months, or even years, but remember what the Word of God says.

> **"...Weeping may endure for a night, but joy comes in the morning."**
>
> **Psalm 30:5b (AMP)**

You may have to talk to a godly counselor, friend, or whoever God leads you to. However long it takes, remember to make going to God your top priority!

"...and there is a friend that sticketh closer than a brother."

Proverbs 18:24b (KJV)

"...and his name shall be called Wonderful, Counsellor, The mighty God, The everlasting Father, The Prince of Peace."

Isaiah 9:6c (KJV)

Please do not hide your pain on the inside; it will only lead to a very vindictive attitude, causing you to seek revenge. Harboring pain can result in explosive behavior, and only God knows what that will lead to. Sheltering your pain will cause you to be very judgmental, blaming everyone else for your pain, even if it's not their fault. This, loved one, is sin. You *cannot* and *will not* get healed by doing these negative things.

God is working on each of us every day. You must know He loves you so much. Even in the midst of your pain, He is working to bring healing. It's important that you allow healing to come His way and in His timing, which is always the right way.

This means you must receive His love and help, and the love and help that He sends our way through others.

Listen and understand this. Even though someone, a few people, or even many people may have done you wrong, you do not have to sin by getting revenge or doing something you know is not right. You've heard the saying, "two wrongs don't make a right". Don't allow yourself to get out of the will of God through sin. Jesus can relate to everything you have gone through in the past, what you are experiencing now and even what lays ahead in your future, yet He did not sin.

> **"For we do not have a High Priest Who is unable to understand and sympathize and have a shared feeling with our weaknesses and infirmities and liability to the assaults of temptation, but One Who has been tempted in every respect as we are, yet without sinning."**
> **Hebrews 4:15 (AMP)**

Loved one, if you turn to Jesus and the help He provides, you will not sin intentionally. He will continue to heal you, and you will always experience the pain that heals.

> **"Now to Him Who is able to keep you without stumbling or slipping or falling, and to present**

[you] unblemished (blameless and faultless) before the presence of His glory in triumphant joy and exultation [with unspeakable, ecstatic delight]."

Jude 24 (AMP)

Scenario 3
Helping a Student

The bell rings and the students come in to Wanda's high school English class.

Wanda: *"Come in everyone, we're going to pick up where we left off yesterday."*

Wanda begins teaching and asking questions. She notices that Karen, one of her smartest students who always raises her hand to answer questions, is not even trying to respond. As a matter of fact, she really isn't into the lesson like she normally would be.
Eventually the bell rings and it is time for the students to go to the last class of the day. Before Karen walks out, Wanda tells her they need to talk briefly.

Wanda: *"Okay Karen, what's going on with you?"*

Karen doesn't say anything, she just looks down.

Wanda (softly): *"Karen, look at me. You can talk to me."*

Karen: *"Ms. Wanda, I'm scared and I don't know what to do."*

Wanda: *"What are you scared of Karen?"*

Karen: *"Are you sure you're not going to tell anyone?"*

Wanda: *"Karen, you have nothing to worry about."*

Wanda reassures her as she begins to cry.

Karen: *"Ms. Wanda. I'm pregnant. I don't understand how I could have done this to myself. I'm an honor student. I planned on getting a scholarship, and going to college. I want to be a high school English teacher like you. And...and...."*

Wanda: *"It's okay...keep going."*

Karen: *"And my parents are going to be so upset. They were so happy about my grades and my goals."*

Karen cries even harder now. Wanda hugs her, remembering she went through the same thing, but instead made a decision that she has regretted her entire life. As she comforts Karen, her mind begins to take her back...

It was a Friday evening. They were out bowling, joking around and having fun when a pregnant woman walked in with her husband. Wanda instantly stops laughing and begins to stare at the couple, especially the young lady.

Bill: *"Okay Wanda, what's going on with you girl? Why haven't you laughed at any of my jokes?"*

Wanda: *"Bill...we need to talk."*

Bill stops laughing and teasing Wanda.

Bill: *"Wanda we are having so much fun, do we have to get serious now?"*

Wanda: *"I'm sorry Bill, but yes."*

Bill: *"Okay Wanda, what's bothering you?"*

Wanda: *"Bill...Bill...I think I'm pregnant."*

Bill: *"What!...I thought you were taking..."*

Wanda: *"I was Bill, but I missed a few days."*

Bill: *"A few days?! A few days!! Wanda, you should have let me know, when you missed one day. I would have worn a condom!"*

There is a silence. Bill tries to calm himself as Wanda begins to cry.

Bill: *"Okay, I have to calm down. Uh...we can still have it."*

Wanda: *"I'm sorry Bill. I've ruined everything for us. Our goals, our hopes, our dreams..."*

Bill: *"No Wanda. That's not true. This is unexpected, but we still can have dreams and goals, we just will have a little one to include, that's all."*

Wanda: *"No! That wasn't the plan. I'm not ready for my mother to be my child's grandmother anyway. She stays drunk! And I wouldn't make a good mother now either."*

Bill: *"Yes you will, Wanda, we can work something out."*

There is a silence.

Wanda: *"Bill there's only one other thing to do."*

Bill: *"I...I don't think we should even consider abortion Wanda."*

There is a silence.

Wanda: *"Bill just this one time. We won't need to worry about babysitters, diapers, and all the stuff that comes with having a baby. Come on… We can still be together and our dreams will still come true."*

Bill is silent. He gets up and paces the floor.

Bill: *"I don't agree with you Wanda. I don't feel good about this at all."*

Wanda: *"Bill…I'm so scared."*

That following week they were at the clinic, scared and unsure, but they still went through with the abortion. As she lay on the table, Wanda told herself that she was making the best choice for the two of them, her mother, and her sister. She already had to watch after her sister, because her mother stayed drunk and slept around with different men. A baby would just add more to her problems.

Now today, Wanda believes that's why Bill listened to his family and decided to date other women. It wasn't because she was the only girl he dated and seriously loved. It was because the girl he seriously loved aborted his child, and that girl just happened to be Wanda.

Wanda regrets her decision up to this very day. She doesn't want Karen to make the same mistake and live with the same regret. Wanda begins to gather her thoughts and looks down at Karen with tears in her eyes.

Wanda: *"Karen, have your baby."*

Karen: *"What?"*

Wanda: *"HAVE YOUR BABY!"*

Karen: *"But I'm scared. I don't have a job, my parents won't be able to babysit, they work, I won't be able to finish high school and go to college...and ..."*

Wanda: *"Karen, I will help you. I will babysit for you. You can take evening classes if necessary. Just know I am here for you, okay?"*

Karen: *"Thank you so much Ms. Wanda!"*

Karen wipes her face and gives Wanda a big hug as the final bell rings.

Karen: *"Can you come to my house when I tell my parents, and let them know you are willing to help out?"*

Wanda: *"Sure baby. Now you go on home so your parents won't be looking for you okay?"*

Karen: *"Okay!! Thanks again Ms. Wanda, and...and.... I love you!!"*

Wanda watches with tears in her eyes as Karen runs down the hall and out the door in pure excitement.
That evening, Wanda soaks in her bubble bath, thinking about Karen and their conversation earlier that day. Then she thinks about how she felt after her ten-year high school reunion. She remembers how she acted towards her mother at the family reunion.

She begins to evaluate her past, what she's gone through, and how it has affected her life, her attitude, and the wrong choices she made in life. She realizes that in order to help Karen, she needs to get some help for herself. All of a sudden, Wanda begins to pray softly.

Wanda: *"Lord, I don't know what to do and I need your help. I'm mad at the world and everyone who has ever hurt me, especially my mother and Bill. I feel like my mother should have been a real mother, and not get drunk so much and sleep with so many different men. I feel like Bill should have still stayed with me and loved me in spite of the abortion. I thought he would understand me, if no one else did. But I'm also mad at myself because I had an abortion".*

The tears start to flow the more she opens her heart to the Lord.

Wanda: *"Lord, I no longer want to pretend like I'm fine, when I'm not. I don't want to lie about it either. So please Lord forgive me and give me the heart to forgive others. Teach me how to walk in forgiveness and your unconditional love so that I can love people the way you love them, no matter what they say to me, or no matter what they may do to me. LORD, PLEASE HELP ME NOW! PLEASE SAVE ME! PLEASE DELIVER ME! I NEED YOU LORD, I NEED YOU!"*

Now she is truly sobbing. Just then there is a knock at the door.

Michael: *"You're not drowning in there are you?"*

She wipes her tears and starts laughing.

Wanda: *"No honey, you can come in."*

Michael comes in and looks in her eyes, again noticing they are red.

Michael: *"Wanda, are you okay? Baby your eyes are red. You didn't get soap in them again did you?"*

This time Wanda looks calmly into her husband's eyes.

Wanda: *"No baby. I need help. I need to go to Christian counseling and I need to tell you the truth. Can we talk?"*

She begins to cry again. He looks into her eyes and touches her face.

Michael: *"Wanda baby, I'm here for you. I'm not going anywhere, and you can talk to me about anything."*

Chapter Three

The Origin of Pain

Where does pain come from? Why do we have to even go through pain? Why is the pain that many of us endure still there when we did not even inflict it upon ourselves? Why do we tend to hurt other people, though many times we don't want to?

These are a few of the many questions that have come into my mind from time to time, and I'm sure you can relate to asking yourself one or more of the same questions. When we're talking about pain, we must deal with its origin, how it actually came into existence in this world.

> **"In the beginning God created the heaven and the earth."**
>
> **Genesis 1:1 (KJV)**

> **"And God saw every thing that he had made, and, behold, it was very good..."**
>
> **Genesis 1:31a (KJV)**

This means there were no flaws or mistakes in anything God created. Everything was perfect and nothing harmful or painful even existed on earth. God created male and female too. Now God gave the male, named Adam, some simple instructions.

"So God created man in his own image, in the image of God created he him; male and female created he them."

Genesis 1:27 (KJV)

"And the LORD God took the man, and put him into the garden of Eden to dress it and to keep it. And the LORD God commanded the man, saying, Of every tree of the garden thou mayest freely eat: But of the tree of the knowledge of good and evil, thou shalt not eat of it: for in the day that thou eatest thereof thou shalt surely die."

Genesis 2:15-17 (KJV)

God told Adam not to eat of one tree, the tree of the knowledge of good and evil. God warned him, if he did not obey, he would surely die; which meant for the first time, Adam would experience pain.

God formed Adam by hand and he became a living soul (Genesis 2:7). Then he was given these instructions in Genesis 2:15-17. However, Eve was taken from Adam's rib, and was called woman, further down in the scriptures (Genesis 2:21-23) Eve clearly didn't come into existence until after Adam received these instructions from God.

"Now the serpent was more subtil than any beast of the field which the LORD God had made. And

he said unto the woman, Yea, hath God said, Ye shall not eat of every tree of the garden? And the woman said unto the serpent, We may eat of the fruit of the trees of the garden: But of the fruit of the tree which is in the midst of the garden, God hath said, Ye shall not eat of it, neither shall ye touch it, lest ye die. And the serpent said unto the woman, Ye shall not surely die: For God doth know that the day ye eat thereof, then your eyes shall be opened, and ye shall be as gods, knowing good and evil."

Genesis 3: 1-5 (KJV)

Eve listened to the serpent, which was the devil. She entertained what he said—deciding he was right instead of God—ate the fruit and gave it to her husband Adam. Adam also disobeyed God by listening to his wife and eating the forbidden fruit.

"And when the woman saw that the tree was good for food, and that it was pleasant to the eyes, and a tree to be desired to make one wise, she took of the fruit thereof, and did eat, and gave also unto her husband with her; and he did eat."

Genesis 3:6 (KJV)

"...Hast thou eaten of the tree, whereof I commanded thee that thou shouldest not eat? And the man said, The woman whom thou gavest to be with me, she gave me of the tree, and I did eat. And the Lord God said unto the woman, What is this that thou hast done? And the woman said, The serpent beguiled me, and I did eat."

Genesis 3:11b-13 (KJV)

This is the point where pain enters the world, through Adam and Eve's disobedience. The serpent was punished also.

"And the LORD God said unto the serpent, Because thou hast done this, thou art cursed above all cattle, and above every beast of the field; upon thy belly shalt thou go, and dust shalt thou eat all the days of thy life: And I will put enmity between thee and the woman, and between thy seed and her seed; it shall bruise thy head, and thou shalt bruise his heel. Unto the woman he said, I will greatly multiply thy sorrow and thy conception; in sorrow thou shalt bring forth children; and thy desire shall be to thy husband, and he shall rule over thee. And unto Adam he said, Because thou hast hearkened unto the voice of thy wife, and hast eaten of the tree, of which I commanded thee, saying, Thou shalt not eat of it: cursed is the ground for thy sake; in sorrow shalt thou eat of it all the days of thy life; Thorns also and thistles shall it bring forth to thee; and thou shalt eat the herb of the field; In the sweat of thy face shalt thou eat bread, till thou return unto the ground; for out of it wast thou

taken: for dust thou art, and unto dust shalt thou return."

Genesis 3:14-19 (KJV)

"Therefore the LORD God sent him forth from the garden of Eden, to till the ground from whence he was taken."

Genesis 3:23 (KJV)

After reading all of this, I'm sure you have figured out that the origin of pain is sin. When Adam and Eve disobeyed God, they sinned against God and caused pain to come upon themselves and the rest of humanity. Yes, Adam and Eve brought sin into this world and therefore we are all born into this world as sinners.

"Behold, I was shapen in iniquity; and in sin did my mother conceive me."

Psalm 51:5 (KJV)

Their disobedience led to much of what we suffer today, such as: labor pains in childbearing (Genesis 3:16), struggles in our marriages (Genesis 3:16), pain from hard work (Genesis 3: 17-19), and experiencing the loss of a loved one (Genesis 3:19).

Then again, thanks be to God that He sent His only begotten Son Jesus to die on the cross for our sins and free us from the bondage that pain brings.

"For God so loved the world, that he gave his only begotten Son, that whosoever believeth in him should not perish, but have everlasting life."

John 3:16 (KJV)

Loved one, it's important to know we are all affected by generations of pain. Adam and Eve's disobedience was humanity's introduction to pain, but we also have origins of pain in our own family line, which means each of us are by-products of pain. Either we have gone through in the past, are experiencing it right now, or will suffer some sort of pain later on in our lives.

Pain that has been passed down through family lineage is called generational pain, or *generational curses*. These can only be broken through the blood of Jesus Christ. This happens when the generation before truly repents of that curse (pain from sin), by confessing it, and completely allowing the love of Jesus Christ to turn their lives around. When this is done, it will not pass on down the line. The next generation may be faced with it, but because it was destroyed in the previous line, it will also be destroyed in their children's lives, and in their children, and so on.

Chapter Four

By-Products of Pain

Living through the consequences of pain is very difficult, but we all have been born into a painful situation and have experienced some sort of pain in our lives. It may have been mental, social, emotional, physical, or spiritual pain. Many have felt different types at the same time, because pain in one area of our lives tends to cross over into another.

For instance, people who are stressed out from worry—mental pain—tend to experience physical aches and pain in their bodies as well. They can have ulcers, high blood pressure, extreme headaches, and sometimes even eating disorders. Someone who has suffered physical pain from abuse may have the same symptoms as a person with mental pain. Also, when someone endures physical pain, it tends to affect their mental and emotional state as well. That person has very low self-esteem and self abuse comes into play, as they somehow blame themselves for the abuse that has been inflicted upon them, which clearly shows a state of emotional pain.

Now spiritual pain is a result of your soul—your very being, who you really are—being wounded. When this happens, this pain increases inactivity in your life, and if not healed can nearly destroy you.

"The thief cometh not, but for to steal, and to kill, and to destroy: I am come that they might have life, and that they might have it more abundantly."

John 10:10 (KJV)

Since sin is the origin of pain, the purpose of pain is to bring the same results as sin. It's meant to steal from you, kill your spirit, and destroy your soul; but Jesus came to clean up what Adam and Eve messed up. He came so you can have life, and live your life to the fullest, both here on earth and in heaven. In order for you to live life to the fullest, more abundantly, you cannot let your pain cause you to sin. You must allow God to heal you so you can help someone else.

Before you can help anyone else, you must first face the truth that we are all by-products of pain. Ask God to reveal the true source of the pain that has become sin in your life. Be honest with yourself: what pain has been passed down from generation to generation (generational curses) and become a part of my life? Ask yourself, what pain am I personally responsible for in my own life and in the lives of others? Most importantly, you must ask God to forgive all your sins. His grace will teach you how to turn away from those sins in the midst of hard times. Only then can you receive His forgiveness. Next, thank Him for all He has shown and taught you, making sure you forgive yourself and others who have played a part in your pain and your sins. Then you can trust God by moving forward and allowing the indwelling power of the Holy Spirit to do the rest.

> **"Likewise the Spirit also helpeth our infirmities: for we know not what we should pray for as we ought: but the Spirit itself maketh intercession for us with groanings which cannot be uttered. And he that searcheth the hearts knoweth what is the mind of the Spirit, because he maketh intercession for the saints according to the will of God."**
>
> **Romans 8:26-27 (KJV)**

Once you run out of counselors, family members and friends to talk to, and there are no words left when you get on your knees, there may be times when all you can do is moan and cry out to God. Just remember the Holy Spirit takes over and continues to pray for you in the midst of all of your pain. Take comfort in knowing Jesus is praying for you continually.

> **"Wherefore he is able also to save them to the uttermost that come unto God by him, seeing he ever liveth to make intercession for them."**
>
> **Hebrews 7:25 (KJV)**

Be encouraged and know that even though you are a by-product of pain, you cannot and will not lose in this Christian walk. With God, Jesus, the Holy Ghost, a host of heavenly angels, and those He uses to help you, you will conquer your pain. You will win!

"And they overcame him by the blood of the Lamb, and by the word of their testimony..."

Revelation 12:11a (KJV)

Chapter Five

Confronting Your Pain Head-On

Now that you realize we are all by-products of pain, and have discovered which generational pains were passed on to became a part of your daily life, it's time to face it head-on.

Facing your pain head-on simply means you are willing to admit it exists in your life. Even though that is a simple task, it is one of the hardest things for us as human beings to do. It's very hard for us to admit that alcoholism runs in our family, or that adultery, divorce, gossiping and backbiting, rage and violence or even lying runs in our family too.

You know why it's so hard to admit these things? Because it forces you to acknowledge you have some of those very same symptoms and attributes in your own personality. When trouble comes your way and life seems overbearing, avoiding the pain and failing to turn to Jesus for help invites those hidden pains to surface. This allows them to overtake you through sin, ultimately bringing destruction to your life.

When the Lord reveals your private issues, buried pains, hidden sins and where they came from, you no longer have an excuse to knowingly and willfully fall into that sin ever again.

"Christ hath redeemed us from the curse of the law, being made a curse for us: for it is written,

Cursed is everyone that hangeth on a tree."

Galatians 3:13 (KJV)

When Jesus died on the cross for your sins He became a curse on your behalf, so you do not have to live under any curse. This means, **you no longer have an excuse.** No longer can you take your pain out on someone else, or run and turn to people, places, and things that are harmful, that will eventually hurt you and others around you. That's why it's so important to stop and pray when you feel the pressure of pain rising up within you. You must stay prayerful, and when you feel too weak to pray, just call on the Name of Jesus and He will come through.

I've been through some very painful situations in my life. Growing up, I witnessed the adults who had an impact on my life make some very poor choices, and I eventually made those same bad choices, even though I promised myself that I wouldn't. In the midst of all the pain I suffered and endured, I learned to call on the name of Jesus, and I'm still learning to do so today. I've also learned He always had someone praying for me, and if it wasn't for their prayers, I wouldn't be here today.

I keep stressing the point that He always has someone praying for you because He is a God that when His people pray, He listens. More importantly, He will respond by showing us certain people's faces, telling us to pray for them, without us even understanding why. So be encouraged, God sees you and is waiting to hear from you.

> **"If my people, which are called by my name, shall humble themselves, and pray, and seek my face, and turn from their wicked ways; then will I hear from heaven, and will forgive their sin, and will heal their land."**
>
> **II Chronicles 7:14 (KJV)**

I believe that we as people need each other--for prayer, comfort and encouragement--in order for us to experience the pain that heals. So, loved one, confront your pain head-on and without fear and know that God is with you during your healing process.

> **"Confess to one another therefore your faults (your slips, your false steps, your offenses, your sins) and pray [also] for one another, that you may be healed and restored [to a spiritual tone of mind and heart]. The earnest (heartfelt, continued) prayer of a righteous man makes tremendous power available [dynamic in its working].**
>
> **James 5:16 (AMP)**
>
> **"....for he hath said, I will never leave thee, nor forsake thee."**

Hebrews 13:5c (KJV)

Chapter Six

Conquer Your Pain by Speaking the Word

Each and every individual in the Bible had to conquer some sort of pain in their lives. Many of them had to overcome multiple pains, but Jesus suffered for all of our pains and conquered them all.

> **"Who hath believed our report? and to whom is the arm of the LORD revealed? For he shall grow up before him as a tender plant, and as a root out of a dry ground: he hath no form nor comeliness; and when we shall see him, there is no beauty that we should desire him. He is despised and rejected of men; a man of sorrows, and acquainted with grief: and we hid as it were our faces from him; he was despised, and we esteemed him not. Surely he hath borne our griefs, and carried our sorrows: yet we did esteem him stricken, smitten of God, and afflicted. But he was wounded for our transgressions, he was bruised for our iniquities: the chastisement of our peace was upon him; and with his stripes we are healed."**
>
> **Isaiah 53:1-5 (KJV)**

Loved one, I'm not naïve to the fact that we live in a world full of pain. Every time you look at the news you see one painful situation after another. All of us encounter painful circumstances in our homes, in our churches, on our jobs and in our communities but we must know within our hearts that the word of God still stands true and the word of God still works.

What does that mean? In the midst of all the pain you experience here on earth God has promised to keep you in perfect peace, if your mind is stayed upon Him (Isaiah 26:3). In the midst of losing your job, He is a present help in the time of trouble (Psalm 46:1). In the midst of your car being repossessed, and your home going into foreclosure, God will supply all your need according to His riches in glory (Philippians 4:19). In the midst of people turning their back on you, He is a comforter (John 14:16,18) and a friend (Proverbs 18:24). In the midst of confusion and an uncertain path, He will order your steps (Psalm 37:23). In the midst of financial decline and difficulty in your life, He will give you the desires of your heart (Psalm 37:4).

You see loved one, conquering your pain doesn't mean it will no longer exist in your life. Nor does it mean you won't be reminded of your painful past, because believe me, even when you try to forget, there will always be someone around to remind you or you will come across someone from the past who has hurt you. Even once you've moved on, you will eventually end up in a situation that reminds you of the past, or you may meet someone new that reminds you of that one who hurt you.

Therefore, conquering your pain means taking a firm stand and deciding when that painful memory comes to overtake you and cause you to sin, you must speak the Word of God! You have to know and believe that you have the victory over your painful past. Speaking God's word is declaring that whatever happened in the past is behind and you are moving forward.

> **"I do not consider, brethren, that I have captured and made it my own [yet]; but one thing I do [it is my one aspiration]: forgetting what lies behind and straining forward to what lies ahead, I press on toward the goal to win the [supreme and heavenly] prize to which God in Christ Jesus is calling us upward."**
> **Philippians 3:13-14 (AMP)**

In this context, forgetting means to release; to literally "let go." Paul is saying in this scripture that I'm letting go of what's in the past; no longer will I allow my past to get me down or hold me back from what God has for my future. Paul said he would press toward his future. To press means to apply pressure to something that is resistant.

Loved one, your past is very resistant. It frequently invades your thoughts, trying to pull your mind back to how you used to act, speak and think. So, like Paul, you need to press toward your future. Release the past. You can't change it, but you can determine the direction your future will take. Press your way through. Change your mind set by reading and speaking the Word of God. Push past the pain right into your future and all the things God has in store just for you.

This reminds me of the scripture about the woman who had an issue of blood for twelve long years. She pressed her way through the crowd surrounding Jesus to touch the hem of His garment so she could be made whole.

And a certain woman, which had an issue of blood twelve years, And had suffered many things of many physicians, and had spent all that she had, and was nothing bettered, but rather grew worse, When she had heard of Jesus, came in the press behind, and touched his garment. For she said, If I may touch but his clothes, I shall be whole. And straightway the fountain of her blood was dried up; and she felt in her body that she was healed of that plague. And Jesus, immediately knowing in himself that virtue had gone out of him, turned him about in the press, and said, Who touched my clothes? And his disciples said unto him, Thou seest the multitude thronging thee, and sayest thou, Who touched me? And he looked round about to see her that had done this thing. But the woman fearing and trembling, knowing what was done in her, came and fell down before him, and told him all the truth. And he said unto her,

Daughter, thy faith hath made thee whole; go in peace, and be whole of thy plague.

Mark 5:25-34 (KJV)

What resistance did she face concerning her difficult past and her present state? It was her disease. It was the frustrating memory of going to see doctor, after doctor, after doctor, and all saying the same thing: there was nothing they could do to help. It was realizing she'd spent all the money she had on doctors that not only couldn't help, but made her condition even worse. It was the pain from isolation, knowing she couldn't be around anybody because her constant bleeding made her unclean; no one wanted to be around her. Yet she pushed past all that pain and pressed through the crowd anyway, which was another form of resistance: the crowd. Others were trying to see Jesus that day, and many touched Him. But he felt *her* touch.

Her touch was different from anyone else's touch in the crowd. Why? In spite of her painful, sickly past and current situation, she believed her future was bright and that Jesus could give that to her. Because she pressed her way through and stepped out on faith, she received what she believed and she was made whole.

Fight for your future! When you really believe the word of God in your heart and speak His word in confidence—knowing what you have spoken will surely come to pass in Jesus' name—Jesus will feel *your* touch, and He will make you whole.

> **"And it shall come to pass, that before they call I will answer; and while they are yet speaking, I will hear."**
>
> **Isaiah 65:24 (KJV)**

Chapter Seven

Be Still and Know

What does it mean to be still? It means to be calm, peaceful, restful, and in a state of tranquility. Now I know from experience that when you are going through some painful times in your life, it is hard to have peace and tranquility. Jesus had peace and tranquility in the midst of a storm. Yet, in this scripture, the disciples panicked, which is how we tend to respond to the storms in our everyday lives.

> **And there arose a great storm of wind, and the waves beat into the ship, so that it was now full. And he was in the hinder part of the ship, asleep on a pillow: and they awake him, and say unto him, Master, carest thou not that we perish? And he arose, and rebuked the wind, and said unto the sea, Peace, be still. And the wind ceased, and there was a great calm.**
> **Mark 4:37-39 (KJV)**

Okay before I move on, I know you may be thinking, *"That was Jesus, and He was and still is perfect."* You are right about that. However, when Jesus came from heaven to walk in His earthly body, He still struggled with the very same feelings we experience today. He could have sinned, allowing the storm to make Him bitter, unforgiving, and full of unrest, but He didn't. Now make no mistake, when Jesus came here on earth, even though He was all God, He was all human too. He knew how it felt to be angry, which is why He tells us:

"Be ye angry, and sin not: let not the sun go down upon your wrath: Neither give place to the devil."

Ephesians 4:26-27 (KJV)

Jesus is letting us know that we are going to get angry, but we don't have to sin. If you allow your anger to reach the point of sin, through unforgiveness and a desire to hurt others, the devil will steal your joy and peace in life. Had Jesus allowed the devil to cause Him to sin, He would have not been able to die on the cross for our sins.

Unfortunately, we take for granted the pain Jesus endured for us. No matter how many times we read the Bible, we tend to think Jesus' walk on earth was easier than ours and that His death wasn't as difficult to endure because He was both God and man. We rationalize He had some superhuman inner strength that kept Him from experiencing the full level of pain, using that as a way to make excuses for our own sins.

What Jesus went through was a horrible pain that we cannot even begin to understand. Not only was He misunderstood and hated by church leaders, but His own family members and closest friends rejected and abandoned Him. He didn't have to suffer on our behalf, yet he loved us enough to willingly lay down His life. We will never truly know the capacity of suffering Jesus endured for us. No matter how much pain we experience in this life, it can never compare.

> **"Wherefore Jesus also, that he might sanctify the people with his own blood, suffered without the gate."**
>
> **Hebrews 13:12 (KJV)**

> **"Then saith he unto them, My soul is exceeding sorrowful, even unto death: tarry ye here, and watch with me. And he went a little farther, and fell on his face, and prayed, saying, O my Father, if it be possible, let this cup pass from me: nevertheless not as I will, but as thou wilt."**
>
> **Matthew 26:38-39 (KJV)**

> **"Thinkest thou that I cannot now pray to my Father, and he shall presently give me more than twelve legions of angels? But how then shall the scriptures be fulfilled, that thus it must be?"**
>
> **Matthew 26:53-54 (KJV)**

Yet, in the midst of all the pain Jesus endured, He tapped into the love of God, His Father, and the love He has for us

(John 3:16). It was the power of the Holy Spirit that allowed Him to endure the suffering until the very end, just for us. My friend, THAT IS UNCONDITIONAL LOVE!

> **"Looking unto Jesus the author and finisher of our faith; who for the joy that was set before him endured the cross, despising the shame, and is set down at the right hand of the throne of God. For consider him that endured such contradiction of sinners against himself, lest ye be wearied and faint in your minds."**
>
> **Hebrews 12:2-3 (KJV)**

To be still doesn't mean you won't feel the impact of your pain. It doesn't mean you won't become angry, upset, nervous, and even scared about some situations that may arise in your life. It simply means now that God lives in your heart, you can tap into the power of His love through His Holy Spirit. Right in the midst of what you're going through you can experience the peace of God that surpasses all understanding.

> **"Be careful for nothing; but in every thing by prayer and supplication with thanksgiving let your**
>
> **requests be made know unto God. And the peace of God, which passeth all understanding, shall keep your hearts and minds through Christ Jesus."**

Philippians 4:7 (KJV)

Once you pass through the storm(s), people will wonder and ask you, *"How did you go through that, and still come out loving God? How is it that you still are so nice to people, when people have lied, cheated, and talked about you?"* People will remind you of the times they saw you cry, get angry, had a temper tantrum or almost had a nervous breakdown; yet they will see you're still praising God. They will see you're still confronting the issues in your life in love because you want to be right with God. People will notice you don't even look like what you've been through, and just like one of my beautiful mentors always says, you'll declare "TO GOD BE THE GLORY!"

You can tell them you tapped into something the world cannot give. It wasn't religion, it wasn't education, it wasn't a human relationship here on earth, but rather the unconditional love of Jesus Christ. Only in Him can you find love, joy, peace, longsuffering, gentleness, goodness, faith, meekness and temperance (Galatians 5:22-23). You will be a living testimony that God's love is real and Jesus is still alive: loving, saving, and healing whoever will receive him.

"Come unto me, all ye that labour and are heavy laden, and I will give you rest."

Mat. 11:28 (KJV)

"Come unto Me, all you who labor and are heavy-laden and overburdened, and I will cause you to rest. [I will ease and relieve and refresh your souls.]

Mat. 11:28 (AMP)

Chapter Eight

It Is Finished

Now before I get into this chapter, I don't want you to have the impression that pain is finished. As mentioned earlier in this book, as long as we exist on this earth, pain will continue to play a part in our lives. However, I do believe you can get to a place in your life where pain doesn't cause you to sin against yourself, against others, and most importantly, against God. I do believe the more you tap into the love of God on a daily basis, you will dispense His love towards other people no matter how they treat you. Again, I'm not saying what people say or do will never affect you, because that's not true. You just don't have to allow what they say or do cause you to sin.

You see, we all look for a way out from time to time. We all try to find the easiest way to not experience pain in this world. Without realizing it, we sometimes become Christians on the run: running from relationship to relationship, church to church, school to school, job to job, and the list goes on and on and on. The truth of the matter is you can never truly run away from pain.

Everywhere you go in life, you will eventually come across people who dislike you for no reason at all. People will talk about you, will be jealous of you or just don't want you to be happy and succeed in life. These types of people may be co-workers or in your school, your community, your church, your family, and sometimes even in your own home. Still, *you* must decide to not let that pain cause you to sin by becoming unforgiving and bitter and then treating them the same way.

> **"But I say unto you, Love your enemies, bless them that curse you, do good to them that hate you, and pray for them which despitefully use you, and persecute you;"**
> **Matthew 5:44 (KJV)**

You cannot use the pain as an excuse to run away from the situation in which God has placed you, for that is sin. You must continue in your commitment to your spouse, children, extended family, friends, church, school, job, community and your world. You can endure the pain and come out of the storm victorious.

> **"Nay, in all these things we are more than conquerors through him that loved us."**
> **Romans 8:37 (KJV)**

We must not buy into what the world says about pain. What does the world say about pain? I'm glad you asked. The world, with all of its glamour and slick advertising, tells us the easiest way to deal with pain is to avoid it all costs. Can't stand the pain and discomfort of waiting? The world tells you to get what you want NOW. That's why we have so many fast food restaurants. That's why we get in the fastest lane at the gas station, grocery store, clothing store, etc. We don't want to endure longsuffering, even though it is one of the fruits of the Spirit (Galatians 5:22). This world and its economy have conditioned our minds against enduring just about anything; therefore we hate waiting and have little patience, which goes against the Word of God that tells us to wait in many scriptures.

"Lead me in thy truth, and teach me: for thou art the God of my salvation; on thee do I wait all the day."

Psalm 25:5 (KJV)

"Wait on the LORD: be of good courage, and he shall strengthen thine heart: wait, I say, on the Lord."

Psalm 27:14 (KJV)

"My soul, wait thou only upon God; for my expectation is from him."

Psalm 62:5 (KJV)

"But they that wait upon the LORD shall renew their strength; they shall mount up with wings as

eagles; they shall run, and not be weary; and they shall walk, and not faint."
Isaiah 40:31 (KJV)

You must take a stand and say, **it is finished in my life; I** will learn how to wait in every area of my life. This world teaches us how to worry and be anxious about many things: losing and gaining weight, starting and ending a relationship, buying material things such as cars, clothes, houses, jewelry, etc. We are constantly bombarded with advertisements telling us we need this or that item, or we need to look like this or that celebrity. Tell the devil he is a liar, and **it is finished**.

Loved one it is time to say **it is finished** and learn to wait on God in the midst of your pain. Whether it's the pain and discomfort of waiting in line at the store, waiting on that wayward child that has lost his way or waiting for that cheating spouse to come home, remember the Lord is with you, even in the midst of your painful wait.

A good example in the word of God is the story of the prodigal son in Luke 15:11-32. His father was in pain, waiting on that lost son to come home, but he didn't use that as an excuse to sin. When his son returned he didn't curse him out, slap him, or beat him up. He received him back with open loving arms, the same way Jesus receives us when we stray from Him. After all, His word says he is married to the backslider (Jeremiah 3:14).

He's not giving us permission to backslide—return to your old ways— in that scripture. He's saying if you find yourself in a backslidden state, don't be ashamed and run from His presence, like Adam and Eve. Don't be like them and make excuses for your sins either (Genesis Chapter 3). When you find yourself in a backslidden state, turn around and run right back into His loving arms, asking for forgiveness.

Remember, He is always waiting with arms wide open, ready for you to come with all of your problems. He already has the solution; He just wants you to trust Him. Before dying on the cross, Jesus' last words were "It is finished" (John 19:30). That means all of the work has already been done and He guarantees your victory. You just need to press your way through to the end.

"Know ye not that they which run in a race run all, but one receiveth the prize? So run, that ye may obtain."

1 Corinthians 9:24 (KJV)

"But he that shall endure unto the end, the same shall be saved."

Matthew 24:13 (KJV)

Chapter Nine

A New Beginning

Scenario 4
The Graduation

Karen is about to graduate from high school. She is excited and very nervous because she is also the valedictorian and has to deliver a speech to her graduating class.

Karen: *"Oooh, Ms Wanda, I am so n-e-r-v-o-u-s.....I hope the words don't stumble out of my mouth."*

Wanda is also excited and nervously zips Karen's gown and adjusts her cap.

Wanda: *"Karen, sweetie, you are going to do great, I promise you that."*

Karen: *"Ms. Wanda, you've always told me that....thank you sooo much, for keeping my baby, when I had to do my homework, and when there was no one else that could keep him at the time. I...I...just don't know what I would have done without you...I love you...and I want to help girls like me too....you know...who are single young mothers...and..."*

They hug and began to cry softly, then Wanda pushes her towards the podium.

Wanda: *"Okay, let me wipe those tears, I hear them calling your name, now get out there and do your thang girl!"*

As Karen approaches the stage, she looks around in amazement and then begins to speak.

Karen: *"Congratulations Class of 2011!! WE MADE IT!!*

The students begin to cheer.

Karen: *"I never thought I would make it this far. But here I am, among all my classmates, family and friends, standing here in amazement of not only being the 2011 valedictorian, but with a four year scholarship to Howard University, which includes living expenses, and childcare for my son.*

The crowd begins to clap again, and then there is a silence as Karen continues.

Karen: *"But I could not have done it alone. Fellow classmates, we are here because of the sacrifices of the people who love us: our parents, our teachers, our counselors, our principal, and even our friends. I want to take the time to tell you who made a great sacrifice for me, other than my parents. Well, I call her Ms. Wanda, my favorite teacher. Ms Wanda, gave me good advice, even when I didn't want to hear it. It is because of her, why I stand here today. Ms. W-a-n-d-a, would you come out here please!"*

The students stand up and cheer for Ms. Wanda, as Karen pulls her out onto the stage.

Later that evening while soaking in the tub, Wanda thinks about the graduation, and the celebration afterwards with the staff and students. Tears roll down her face as she talks to God thanking Him for all He has done in her life. Wanda begins to pray.

Wanda: *"Lord God, I thank you for helping me to move on with my life. I thank you for your healing power that I'm still experiencing right now. You have enabled me to experience the pain that heals, so I can help Karen, who* *is now my god-daughter. I pray that I can continue to be a help to many people. Thank you for renewing my relationship with my mother. Thank you for helping me to forgive Bill. Thank you for helping me to forgive myself for all the wrong decisions I've made in the past. Thank you for helping me realize when I used my pain to lash out and hurt others instead of helping them. Thank you Lord for my husband and children who stayed by my side throughout this whole painful experience. Most importantly thank you Lord, for you, for doing just as your word says. You never left me, and you never gave up on me."*

Just then Wanda's husband knocks on the door.

Michael: *"You're not drowning in there are you?"*

Wanda (laughing): *"No, come on in sweetheart."*

Michael: *"Are you okay baby? Your eyes are red."*

Wanda smiles and gazes right into her husband's eyes.

Wanda: *"Yes baby, I'm absolutely wonderful. I was just thanking God for my....Karen's....all of our new beginnings."*

"Remember ye not the former things, neither consider the things of old. Behold, I will do a new thing; <u>now</u> it shall spring forth..."
Isaiah 43:18-19a (KJV)

The Beginning

Conclusion

The truth of the matter is we all must experience pain in this lifetime. But, we must know our Lord and Savior Jesus Christ knows all about our hurts, our sorrows and our pains. He is always there to comfort us through every painful situation in our lives, if we allow Him.

When you allow Him to comfort, caress, talk to, kiss, embrace and heal you (Isaiah 53)—even through your most difficult times in life—you will begin to see every painful situation He has allowed you to endure, whether through wrong choices or from the tests and trials He sends your way, can and will turn around and work for your own good (Romans 8:28).

He does this by using you to be a blessing and help someone else. Your testimony of perseverance all the way to victory will encourage those who may be experiencing the same pain. Once someone sees how you were able to hold on to your faith and overcome the pain, they realize they too can be healed. When we *truly* realize the *purpose* for all of our pain, then and only then, will we *really* see and experience the **Pain That Heals**.

"The Spirit of the Lord GOD is upon me; because the LORD hath anointed me to preach good tidings unto the meek; he hath sent me to bind up the brokenhearted, to proclaim liberty to the captives, and the opening of the prison to them that are bound; To proclaim the acceptable year of the LORD, and the day of vengeance of our God; to comfort all that mourn; To appoint unto them that mourn in Zion, to give unto them beauty for ashes, the oil of joy for mourning, the garment of praise for the spirit of heaviness; that they might be called trees of righteousness, the planting of the LORD, that he might be glorified."

ISAIAH 61:1-3 (KJV)

Bibliography

Introduction
Romans 3:20-23

Chapter One
Proverbs 3:5-6
Hebrews 4:15
Psalm 46:1
Psalm 121:2
Psalm124:8
Hebrews 4:16
I Peter 5:6

Chapter Two
James 5:16
Isaiah 61:7
Hebrews 10:38
Ecclesiastes 1:9
Proverbs 11:14
Psalm 30:5b
Proverbs 18:24b
Hebrews 4:15
Jude 24

Chapter Three
Genesis 1:1
Genesis 1:31
Genesis 1:27
Genesis 3:17-19

Chapter Three (con't)
John 3:16

Chapter Four
John 10:10
Romans 8:26-27
Hebrews 7:25
Revelation 12:11a

Chapter Five
Genesis 3:13
II Chronicles 7:14
James 5:16
Hebrews 13:5c

Chapter Six
Isaiah 26:3
Psalm 46:1
Philippians 4:19
John 14:16
Proverbs 18:24
Psalms 37:4
Philippians 3:13-14
Genesis 2:15-17
Genesis 2:7
Genesis 2:22
Genesis 3:1-4
Genesis 3:6

Chapter Six (con't)
Genesis 3:11b-13
Genesis 3:14-19
Genesis 3:23
Psalm 51:5
Genesis 3:16

Chapter Seven
Mark 4:37-39
Ephesians 4:26
John 3:16
Philippians 4:7
Matthew 11:28

Chapter Eight
Matthew 5:44
Psalm 25:5
Psalm 27:14
Psalm 62:5
Isaiah 40:31
Luke 15:11-32
Jeremiah 3:14

Conclusion
Isaiah 53
Romans 8:28
Isaiah 61:1-3

www.ingramcontent.com/pod-product-compliance
Lightning Source LLC
Chambersburg PA
CBHW070605180626
46817CB00005B/2008